The Story of Filomena

Book One of "The Adventures of Filomena" Series

Fernando M. Reimers

Acknowledgements
Several friends in various continents read a draft of this story to their children or children in their families and offered suggestions, other friends read a final draft and provided feedback. I thank Mary Frazier-Davis, Maria Paz Dominguez and Valentin, Maria Paz Ferreres and Sofia and Tomas Marcilese, Mitalene Fletcher, Kristin Foster, Andrew, Jordan and Lundy Frishman, Crystal Baer Green, Andrew Ho, Armida Lizárraga and Isabel Bird Lizárraga, Nell O'Donnell-Weber, Matt and Rosie Weber, Maria Elena Ortega, Carlos Reimers, Eleonora Villegas-Reimers, Mariana Zamboni Sandoval, Jennifer and Henry Norton, and Rose, Elise, Helen and Elliot Wettstein.

Illustrations: Tanya Yastrebova

Book Layout by Chrissy at Indie Publishing Group

ISBN-13: 978-0692128121 (Fernando Reimers)

ISBN-10: 0692128123

US Library of Congress Control Number: 2018906190

CreateSpace Independent Publishing Platform
North Charleston, South Carolina

This book is dedicated to Pablo and Tomás, who first brought Filomena to our family, and who then taught me to see her with new eyes, when they left her in our care.

The Story of Filomena

My name is Filomena and I live on School Street in a small town near the city of Boston. In the mornings I hear the children as they walk to a school a block away from my house.

My body is covered with blue and white feathers. My wings have many layers of dark blue and grey feathers with a lighter edge, like the waves in a blue ocean.

I have a long feathered tail almost as long as the rest of my body. I have two feet, and four toes on each. When I stand on my perch, two of my toes face forward, and two face backwards. I have claws at the tip of my toes which help me get a very good grip on my perch and to climb all around my cage.

I have two small eyes, one on each side of my head. My shiny yellow beak extends downwards and ends in a pointy tip, which I use to grab seeds and everything I eat. Where the beak is close to my face, it is covered by shiny light blue skin and has two small holes—they are my nose through which I breathe.

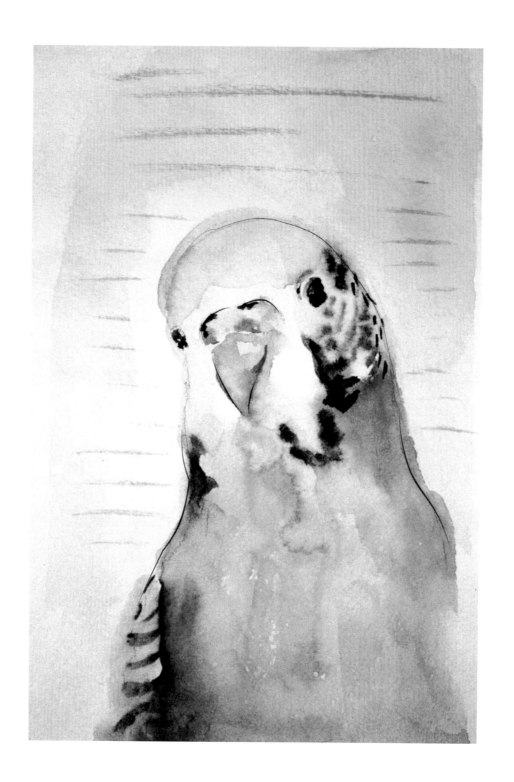

The cage where I live has four perches, two swings, and two doors. At the bottom of the cage, on each side, are two large green plastic feeders. In one of them is the water I drink. In the other is my food, a mix of small seeds, round and shiny, golden, brown and black.

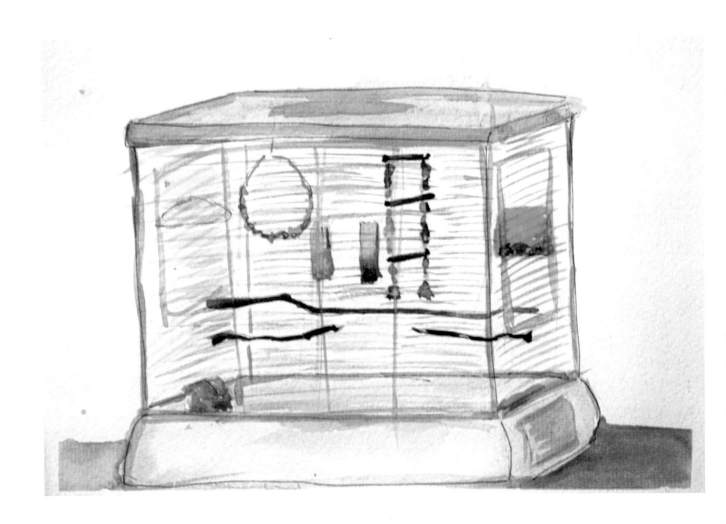

Attached to one of the sides of my cage are two smaller food and water dispensers. They are long plastic cylinders from which food or water move gently to two small cups which I can reach from one of my perches. I prefer to drink and eat from those small feeders rather than from the feeders on the floor of the cage, because it is more comfortable to eat while I stand on my perch than standing on the edge of the feeder on the floor. This is because I don't like my long feathered tail to catch dirt on the floor.

I spend a lot of time jumping in small steps from one end to the other of my favorite perch, a long brown tree branch. The smallest perch is next to a cuttlefish bone where I smooth my beak.

There are two swings hanging from the ceiling of my cage. One is a three-step ladder. The steps are short wooden sticks, attached to two ropes with little wooden beads and blocks. From the bottom step on the ladder hang two small bells which tinkle when I climb the steps of the swing. I love to climb up and down this ladder, and to chew on the wooden beads. The second swing is a circle made of little wooden blocks. I like playing on this swing because it is challenging to keep my balance.

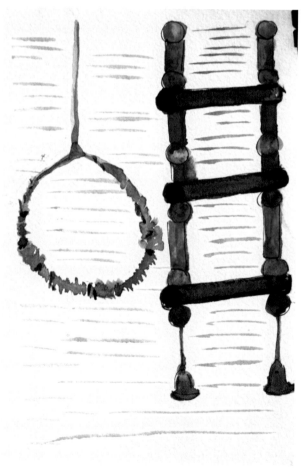

Eleonora and Fernando live in the house with me. Every morning, Fernando comes down to the living room and takes off the blanket that covers my cage at night. He then brings my cage to the kitchen table. He puts fresh water in my two water feeders, and puts seeds in my two food feeders. He gets a big large leaf of romaine lettuce from the refrigerator and clips it to one of the sides of my cage. During the day I will slowly eat it. I love lettuce. Sometimes Fernando will give me a small piece of banana, or pear, or orange, or a cantaloupe, or strawberry. Everyday he gives me a long sprig of millet, one of my favorite foods to eat.

I get excited when Fernando gives me food, so I talk to him. He also talks to me. We speak different languages. He hears me chirp, I hear him say words. He speaks to me in Spanish, and sometimes in English. No matter what language he uses I understand what he says: 'Good morning Filomena, did you sleep well? What are you going to do today?'

After he puts food in my feeders, He puts his hand inside the cage and gently brings his finger close to me. I grab his index finger with one of my claws, and I bite him gently with my beak. I don't bite to hurt him—just to let him know that I want to play. He pretends to be a pirate and tells me: 'Come on little hawk, defend yourself! This is the time of reckoning.' He moves his thumb as if it were the arm of a pirate holding a sword, and I grab his thumb with my beak as if I were grabbing the sword in the hand of the pirate. I know I am not a hawk, I am a parakeet. I also know Fernando is not a pirate, he is a Professor, but we pretend to be a hawk and a pirate fighting in an imaginary pirate ship.

After playing with me Fernando turns on the radio and we listen to some music, while he prepares breakfast. Then Eleonora joins us. I recognize the sound of her steps when she comes down the stairs. Eleonora has a beautiful voice and is very gentle. She asks me how I am doing, and I sing to her to let her know I am happy to see her. Sometimes Eleonora will give me something else to eat, a piece of strawberry or a small piece of pear or a slice of mango. While she and Fernando eat their breakfast I look at them as I am perched on the long branch inside my cage. I look at them carefully, I observe. I see what they do, I listen. Observing and listening helps me know about them and what they do, it helps me learn what they are thinking. You can learn a lot about the world if you observe and listen. Observing is not just looking or seeing, and listening is not just hearing. To observe you have to think about what you see and hear, you have to ask questions.

I have known Eleonora and Fernando for all the eleven years I have lived in this house on School Street. I did not always eat breakfast with them. I was only a year old when I first moved into the house. At that time there were two children in the house, Tomas and Pablo, and they played a lot with me. They spent a lot of their time looking at me and talking to me. They would pet me and sometimes they would take me outside the cage. They also would change the swings in my cage from time to time, which made me very happy.

When I first arrived to the house I was Pablo's parakeet. He would wake me up in the morning, feed me, change my water and talk to me. In the evenings, he would cover my cage with a blanket so I would not be cold when I slept. Then, as Pablo and Tomas grew older, they became busier. They spent most of their day in school. Pablo also spent much time playing basketball. So I would only see them in the evenings when they came to the living room late at night. Sometimes they would let me outside my cage. I would enjoy listening to them talk or watch TV or play video games in the living room.

When Tomas finished high school, five years ago, he left for college and the living room became a little more quiet. Pablo would play guitar in the evenings, and watch basketball games on TV. I enjoyed listening to him play the guitar. Sometimes he would talk to me as we watched basketball games.

Three years ago Pablo went to college too, and so Eleonora and Fernando began to spend more time with me. Maybe they thought I would be lonely now that Tomas and Pablo had left the house. I do miss them, and love when they come home to visit.

After Eleonora and Fernando eat their breakfast in the morning they read the newspaper. Sometimes they talk about the news they are reading. I wish they taught me how to read so I could follow what they are talking about. Then they leave the house to go to work. They are both Professors who teach in universities.

When Eleonora and Fernando are away during the day I sing in my cage. I also listen to the music on the radio. In the middle of the afternoon I hear the children passing by our house as they return from school.

I exercise a lot. I climb the walls of my cage. Sometimes I climb the rooftop of my cage, hanging from the top, with my head looking down. I swing on my swing sets. I like the tinkling of the bell when I climb on the ladder. I also groom myself when I am on my perch. I can preen my feathers with my beak. I pass each feather through my beak to straighten them and keep them clean. My neck is very flexible and I can turn my head backwards and groom the feathers on my back too. When I am cleaning myself I will stretch my wings, one at a time, so I can clean those feathers too. I can spend hours each day preening my feathers.

At the end of the day I hear Eleonora and Fernando talking outside the house as they walk from the car to the kitchen door when they return from work. Fernando opens the back door and comes into the kitchen talking very loudly 'Hello Filomena. How was your day? Did you miss me?' Sometimes he will put his hand inside my cage, and I will grab his finger to play our pirate-hawk game, while we both laugh. I think he misses me when he is outside the house. Eleonora speaks to me much more softly. Her voice is sweet and nice. 'How are you Filomena?' she will say 'Did you eat all your food?' 'Were you lonely?'

Then they cook dinner in the kitchen, and I watch and listen to them from my cage. They talk while they are cooking, and they talk to me too. I observe and listen as they have dinner. After dinner, they do the dishes, and each one of them goes to work on their laptop. Eleonora writes in the living room and Fernando writes at the kitchen table.

Sometimes Eleonora brings me to the living room with her after dinner. She sits on a big sofa in the living room, and takes a lot of papers from a large canvas bag she brings from work next to her. She puts on her glasses and reads these papers, and writes on her laptop. From my cage I see her reading and writing. I like the sound as she presses the keys on her laptop. To get her attention I walk to the side of the cage closer to where she is, I grab the bars of the cage with my toes, flap my wings and chirp at the top of my lungs. She will then look at me and talk to me a little. That makes me feel very happy. And then I keep quiet so she can get back to work. She is reading papers which her students have written. Her students want to be teachers, and Eleonora is helping them prepare to be teachers.

There are other times when, after dinner, I stay at the kitchen table. Fernando sits at the other end of the table and types on his laptop. He writes books. He also reads papers which his students write, and he writes to them. Fernando's students will have jobs to help teachers do their work. Fernando leaves the music on while he is working.

If I call him he does not seem to listen. Even if I yell to the top of my lungs, and flap my wings, he just types and types. I wish I knew how to open my cage, so I could get out and sit on top of his keyboard so he would know I want to play. Sometimes he will realize I am calling him and will get up, open my cage door, get his hand close to me, and we will play our pirate-hawk game. We laugh, and then I let him go. I enjoy listening to the music on the radio as I perch on one leg while I tuck the other underneath my body. If I get tired standing on one leg, I will stand on the other for another while. Taking turns standing on one leg and then the other is relaxing to me. It helps me fall asleep.

Later at night, when he is finished writing, Fernando will bring my cage to the living room. He and Eleonora will watch TV. After that, they will cover my cage with a blanket, turn off the lights, and walk up the stairs to their bedroom. After they turn off the lights the entire house will be dark like the night, it will be so quiet and still, and we will all go to sleep.

I sleep standing on my perch. I know how to keep my balance. I close my eyes, and just sleep.

I love this family. They are my family. The three of us live in a house in School Street in a small town outside the city of Boston.

Questions about the book

What did you like most about this story?

Who is Filomena?

Who does Filomena live with?

What does Filomena do when she wakes up?

What does Filomena do during the day?

What does Filomena do when she is listening to music that is relaxing?

What game does Filomena like to play with Fernando?

What languages does Filomena understand?

Why does Filomena like to observe?

What would you like to know about Filomena?

What do you think Filomena enjoys most doing?

What does Filomena think Professors do when they are at home? Why does she think that?

Who else lived in Filomena's house when she moved in but is no longer there? Why?

What do you think Filomena is wondering about the children who pass the house when they go to school?

What does Filomena wonder about the lives of Eleonora and Fernando when they are not in the house?

Do you have or know someone who has a pet? How do you think that animal sees you? How do they see other children?

Filomena thinks that observing is more than seeing or hearing. Observe carefully something that interests you. What do you observe? How do you know?

36144009R00027

Made in the USA
Middletown, DE
15 February 2019